The Things
I Learned In Life

by
Joel Schwader

In Memory of
Frank (Junior) Schwader

The Things I Learned in Life

Copyright © 1998 by
Joel David Schwader

Revised Edition
2nd Printing 1998
3rd Printing 1999

Cover Photo
Courtesy of Freeman Courier

Library of Congress
Catalog Card Number: 98-90560

ISBN: 1-57579-117-X

Printed in the United States of America

PINE HILL PRESS, INC.
Freeman, S. Dak. 57029

Table of Contents

Foreword	v
Introduction	vii
In Memory of Frank Schwader	ix
Man of Courage	1
My Story	2
A Home Town Stroll	3
Rural Values	4
Family Tree	5
The Old Forgotten Farmstead	6
A Husband and Wife	8
A Mother's Love	9
My First Boss	10
Empty Houses	11
Your Last Name	12
A Mighty Tree	13
First Kiss	14
Father and Friend	16
The Ways of a Friend	17
Thanksgiving	18
Memories of Fall	20
A Prairie Town	21
Signs of the Season	22
The Silent Train	23
A Treasured House	24
Changing Seasons	25
Night Sounds	26
Fishing Daze	27
When Life Unfolds	28
The Gift	29
Hill of Dreams	30

Childhood Memories	32
Take Time	33
Buddy Bunny	34
Winter's Coming	35
Growing Older	36
Best Friends	37
Grandma's House	38
Christmas Time	39
Proud Farmers	40
Our Futures	41
The Duck Hunt	42
Love's Mistake	44
My Little Girl	45
The Childhood Swing	46
Sundays	47
Time Together	48
Lonely and Forgotten	50
Growing Pains	52
Graduation	53
Paying A Visit	54
A Brother's Friend	55
Nothing Stays The Same	56
What Happens To Your Prayers	57
I Know She Misses Dad	59
Someone's Missing	60
My Church	61
A Hero	62
The Blacksmith	63
The Visit	64
Treasured Friend	66
Uncle Paul	67
A Tribute	68
The Goodbye	69
About The Author	70
Comment Page	71

Foreword

It began as a search for solace, then turned into a dream. Joel Schwader of Custer, S.D., who calls himself "The Common Man's Poet" is passionate about promoting family values. His book, The Things I Learned In Life inspires at the same time it issues a call to return to pre-1960s ethics.

It all started at a grief class where the leader encouraged participants to keep a journal as a way of recording the stages in their grief process. Schwader was mourning the death of his father, and his journal was recorded as poetry which started "coming into his head." He has collected the material into a book which will be available at Barnes and Noble, B.J. Dalton and Walden Books.

Tears and laughter, sorrow and joy—these are two sides of a coin for this young man who had his beginnings in Freeman, S.D. It was here that the values he writes about were instilled, first by his father and then by his extended family, the whole town of Freeman.

Schwader's poems are not "preachy" even though they embrace old-fashioned family values. Instead they tug at the heartstrings of common human experiences as they tell about lessons learned from the village blacksmith and a favorite uncle, among others. The poignancy of leaving childhood behind is captured in poems like "The First Kiss" and "Buddy Bunny."

The poetry is almost Wordsworthian in the way it captures the soothing effect of nature on the individual; at the same time it is Whitmanesque in the way it lustily proclaims the innate goodness and individuality of man. Schwader's poetry is like Robert Frost's in his cadences, but he is uniquely himself in the way he melds rhythm and thought.

Schwader has turned from being just a poet to being a man with a mission. He is certain that people are hungry for the lessons he wants to teach. He knows that society can not turn back the clock;

certain conditions have evolved over the past 40 years which he would change if he could. The reality though is that, while he can't change society, he can try to change the human heart.

Schwader himself is a rough-hewn, bearded man. He has been a meat-cutter, a lumber mill worker, and a trapper. He is living proof that adversity doesn't have to keep a man down. Bible oriented, he knows that "heaviness endures for a night, but joy comes in the morning."

His present passion is sharing the things he learned in life, the most significant of which is that joy follows pain. *The Things I Learned In Life* evolved out of the tremendous pain of his father's death; it is perfect proof that sorrow can be transmuted, that joy "comes in the morning." For Schwader, morning has come.

— Dr. Ruth Gossen
Professor of English
Custer, South Dakota

Introduction

My purpose in writing these poems and putting this book together is to help people realize that we can and do learn from each other's pleasant and unpleasant experiences in life. My stories include the loss of a loved one to raising teenagers all while living and growing up in a small midwestern town. The following poems are all lessons we learn in life.

So, please join me as I take you back in time to the town of Freeman, South Dakota and you can follow me through the adventures of growing up and experience the *The Things I Learned in Life.*

— Joel David Schwader
The Common Man's Poet

Photo Courtesy of Freeman Courier

In Memory of Frank Schwader, Jr.

Remember Him

Remember him, the barber, who we caught sleeping in his chair.
    We used to say he napped more than he cut hair.

Remember him, the cook, and how his food would taste.
    When you left the table, there was not a bit of waste.

Remember him, the father, and the spankings that we got.
    Then we'd all go fishing; and we realized that he loved us a lot.

Remember him, the husband, Mom and he were quite a pair.
    Mom was a practicing nurse, and his business was cutting hair.

Remember him, the friend, and all the visits that you had.
    Remember all of this, and you will remember my Dad.

Man of Courage
(Dedicated to my Son, Joshua)

He wore blue jeans and a baseball cap with a little striped shirt.
    He was an average little boy who loved to play in the dirt.

Then one day when he was young, the doctors came to us
    With bad news. They told us "in God's love, put your trust".

They said that he was different, that some parts just weren't made.
    Our son came into this world without sockets for his shoulder blades.

At first, I was stunned, then I said this cannot be.
    My first reaction to the news was the thought "why me".

I cried for the little boy who never could climb trees.
    I cried for the things he would never do with me.

But this little boy was tough; he grew up strong and tall.
    The outlook that he has on life should be a lesson to us all.

He wakes up every morning and says there's nothing I cannot do.
    If the tables were turned in your life, ask yourself, could you.

I've seen him struggle every day, just living with the pain
    Of knowing he is different, that he is not the same.

Looking at this young boy, you'd never know what he's been through.
    There is a man of courage that walks behind those childish eyes of blue.

My Story

There is a method to my madness,
    I tell myself each day.
I just want someone to listen
    to what I have to say.

I want to tell my story
    of what happened long ago,
Of the people, places,
    and the things I used to know.

I would like for you to know
    that life wasn't always this way.
That life was so much simpler
    back in my younger days.

So, listen with your ears
    and follow with your mind,
As I take you on a journey
    somewhere back in time.

A Hometown Stroll

I wanted to take a walk but everyone had gone to bed.
    I needed some cool night air to help me clear my head.

I walked outside the house, then took a look around;
    then I started on my walk through my old hometown.

As I walked down the street, you could hear the locust in the trees.
    The air was cool and crisp; you could feel it in the breeze.

The street lamps lit the corner with a soft and subtle light,
    acting like a beacon and leading me in the night.

Some houses still had lights on, but they went out one by one;
    serving as a sign to me that the day was now forever done.

I walked down the sidewalk under a canopy of trees,
    and shadows danced beside me, made by the moonlight and the leaves.

As I walked along the street, there was a smell that drifted my way.
    Although I could not see it, someone had cut his grass today.

I walked a few more blocks; I had made it to the park.
    And, somewhere in the distance, you could hear a dog begin to bark.

I walked on over to the swing and sat there for a while.
    I thought about my walk and all I did was smile.

For I had come home for a visit and everything had changed.
    But taking this walk tonight proved some things stay the same.

Rural Values

I was born in a rural town; of that I'm proud to say,
    it taught me about life in many different ways.

The way you treat your neighbor, your teacher, and your friend,
    reflects upon your life until the very end.

You treat people with respect and respect the words they say.
    You go to church on Sundays and stop each night to pray.

Values mean a lot in a rural town.
    Friends are friends for life; they never let you down.

And when life knocks you over and treats you so unfair,
    there are always people waiting to say how much they care.

The people of a rural town, they're special and they're neat.
    They are the kind of people someday you'd like to meet.

So, next time that you see someone slowly walking by,
    acting awfully friendly, and saying a quiet "Hi."

I'll bet he's from a rural town and feeling out of place.
    Return the friendly gesture and put a smile upon your face.

Family Tree

My Mother and my Father
    instilled inside of me,
A sense of what it was
    to be part of a family.

They taught me of traditions
    and things that should be done.
They are passed down through the families
    to the parent and their sons,

Like Christmas time and presents,
    the lighting of the tree,
Being with your family
    was the greatest place to be.

The family that I grew up with
    were as close as we could be,
Each of us was a living part
    of our family tree.

If I was granted one wish today,
    I would wish that wish to be,
That every one could be a part
    of a caring family tree.

The Old Forgotten Farmstead

I was supposed to be hunting pheasants;
    it was just the dog and me.
We were rambling through the cornfield
    when I saw this clump of trees.

When I walked out of this cornfield,
    I was greeted by weeds grown high
And saw that hiding in that clump of trees,
    to me, was a grand surprise.

There were buildings old and weathered
    with a faded old red barn.
To me it was a relic of the past;
    it was someone's old, forgotten farm,

I felt like I was traveling,
    if only in my mind.
I was living with these people now
    somewhere back in time.

Then I walked on over to the barn;
    it leaned to some degree.
The only thing that kept it up
    was a mighty cottonwood tree.

I looked inside the door,
    and then a window or two.
Safety was my first concern;
    now what should I do?

Well, I just stood outside
    and looked to see what I could see.
I saw history unfolding
    right in front of me.

In the middle of the barn was a tractor
    that had seen it's better days.
The baler hitched behind it
    was full of rotten hay.

There were tools of every kind
    scattered everywhere.
They were dusty and full of rust;
    not shown a bit of care.

Then I made my way through the weeds
    across the old farmstead,
And imaginings of long ago
    slowly filled my head.

Then I saw that old clothesline
    where they hung their clothes to dry.
The windmill was still standing;
    In the wind, it creaked and sighed.

Then, I walked on over to the house
    and let myself on in.
Windows were broken everywhere; through them,
    you could hear the wind calling
    like a ghost for me to come back again.

Plaster and glass were to be found
    in almost every room,
And in the corner of the kitchen stood
    an old worn out broom.

Then I walked back to my truck,
    by the side of the road, only to see
The old farmstead was gone now.
    It was lost in all the weeds.

I hope it stays that way,
    so that no one ever finds
This lost part of America
    that we have left behind.

A Husband and Wife

Somewhere on a country road back inside my mind,
    I can see a boy and girl in another time.

Holding hands and kissing with love they had to share;
    the boy says, ìI love you, with this ring we'll be a pair.

I see them at the altar now, with friends and family all around,
    inside a little church in a country town.

They took their vows before God to pledge throughout their lives
    that he would be her husband she would be his wife.

The children, they came later; two was all they had.
    The couple now were parents. Their titles were Mom and Dad.

Their lives were never easy; there were problems everywhere.
    But, throughout all the struggle, they stayed together as a pair.

This family never had a fortune and very little fame.
    The legacy they leave behind will be their family name.

A Mother's Love

When I was very young,
    my Mother came to me,
And tried to explain about
    the things that I could not see.

Things I could not see;
    I just don't understand.
She said let's take a walk
    as she grabbed my little hand.

She told me there were gifts
    that were sent down from above.
One of them, she said,
    was called a Mother's love.

A Mother's love you cannot see
    or even understand.
It's something to carry with you
    even when you are a man.

A Mother's love surrounds you
    as you walk the roads of life.
It changes just a little
    when you stop and take a wife.

A Mother's love is special;
    it cares not what you do,
Just as long as you remember
    these three words, I love you.

My First Boss
(Dedicated to Eddie Schamber)

The first time that I saw him,
    he was skinny as a rail.
He looked like an old man
    with his mop and pail.

They said he was my boss,
    that he would teach me what to do.
I thought to myself,
    who would be teaching who.

He taught me things that summer,
    I never will forget.
Twenty years have passed now,
    and I remember them yet.

This old man taught me
    to take pride in what you do.
The way that you do your work
    reflects solely upon you.

He would always tell me
    to work hard every day,
To stop and love your family,
    and don't forget to pray.

Those words of wisdom
    helped me throughout my life.
They are the words that I preach
    to my children and my wife.

Although I never had the chance
    to tell him how I feel,
I hope this poem I wrote for him,
    somehow will.

Empty Houses

The house stands empty;
    the weeds have grown high.
People hardly notice it
    when they drive by.

The paint is chipped;
    the windows are broken everywhere.
The house has been neglected;
    it really needs repair.

People once lived here;
    they gave it life.
A man raised his children
    with his loving wife.

But as families grow,
    so do their dreams.
This house was left
    for other things.

As the years passed by
    and seasons changed,
The house was left empty
    and without a name.

For a house is built for families;
    it's built to be a home.
Without a name attached,
    it only stands alone.

So next time that you see a house
    in disrepair like this,
Stop and think
    of what it missed.

The love and laughter
    with children around
Is what makes a house a home
    in these little towns.

Your Last Name

I was given a gift
    the day that I was born.

It's something that I'll always have;
    it's something to be worn.

My parents gave it to me
    the day that I arrived.

It made my Father happy
    and it made my Mother cry.

I carry it all through my life,
    it's with me every day.

It touches my heritage;
    I cherish it each day.

When I went to marry,
    I gave it to my wife.

She and my children
    will carry it for life.

By now you realize
    the gift was just a name.

That's why I am who I am,
    and we are not the same.

A Mighty Tree

There sits inside my mind,
    a scene of long ago.
The memory of my youth
    and things I used to know,

Far off in a meadow
    and high upon a hill.
There, stands a mighty tree
    that time will never kill.

In my youth, I went there
    to sit among the shade
To think about my life
    and decisions that I'd made.

I would listen to the wind
    blow through the many leaves,
A lullaby it sang
    as if only just to me.

I would climb the branches of the tree
    that spread so far and wide.
At times you'd climb so high
    you could almost touch the sky

Although my years of climbing trees
    are now forever done,
My memories of that time
    will always be of fun.

If I could be granted one more wish,
    I'd wish that wish to be,
That someone very young
    would find that prairie tree.

First Kiss

That night, the best that I can remember,
    was cold for that time of year.
I bundled up in my coat and ventured out
    to confront my fears.

I was going on my first date;
    I would take her to the football game.
As I ventured from the house that night
    I thought Lord, I must be insane.

For I did not know girls,
    and they did not know me.
The only thing my Father said was something
    of the birds and the bees.

He had said this thing called dating is a venture
    you'll do alone.
That night as I went to pick her up,
    I got so scared I ran back home.

I called her up and said,
    "I will meet you at the game."
"Yeah, I'll see you later, good-bye,
    and what's your name?"

Then I went to the game,
    and I looked all around.
I searched through the crowd,
    but my date could not be found.

Then all at once I saw her;
    she was smiling back at me.
Then nervously I approached her
    with my knocking knees.

Lord, the moment, it was awkward;
    oh, just what to say
Then I turned my thought towards the Lord,
    "Please send some help my way."

Then she said, "Let's go get popcorn."
    And the two of us just went
Watching football and eating junk food
    was how our date was spent.

After the game
    I walked her home that night.
This dating, it is easy.
    It is going to be all right.

When we walked up to her front porch,
    I noticed her pretty smile was gone.
She was acting awfully funny,
    like something had gone wrong.

Then all at once, she stepped up
    and kissed me on the lips.
I was so surprised
    that I turned my head and spit.

I was so embarrassed.
    Lord, what should I do?
She broke the ice with these words,
    "Was it your first kiss, too?"

I walked home late that evening
    as a boy on top of the world.
I had made it through my first date
    and even kissed a girl.

Father and Friend

On a hot summer night
    in a country town,
Come the close of the day,
    Dad and I would go sit down.

We'd sit out on the front step
    and watch the daylight end.
He wasn't just my Father;
    he truly was my friend.

I guess that he could tell the times
    when I really needed a friend.
That's when Dad would disappear
    and the title of parent would end.

He never told me
    just exactly what to do.
He would just listen, then say,
    "The decision is up to you."

I could tell him things about my life
    that I could never tell my Dad.
I know it sounds kind of funny,
    but I think it made him glad.

Now that I am older,
    it is time for me to say
That he was the greatest friend
    I've had to this very day.

Now that I am married with children,
    I want to continue what was begun,
I'll be the best friend
    always to my only son.

The Ways Of A Friend

I am my Father's son in every shape and form.
    I've carried his name with me since the day I was born.

He's been there by my side with me every day.
    He's always been a friend to me, what more could I say?

I could say my Dad was tough with me, he never spoiled the child.
    He always had a gentle side that he shared once in a while.

I could say he was a sculptor, my life was but the clay,
    and made me the person that I am today.

I could say he was a gardener, he knew how to make things grow.
    My Father often told me, "You reap exactly what you sow."

I could say my father taught me the ways of a friend.
    You should help them with their burdens and have
    a hand to lend.

I am my Father's legacy; I live it every day
    by the way I treat my neighbors and by the words I say.

Thanksgiving

My father started up the car that cold November day;
    He loaded up the family and we were on our way.

We were headed to my Uncle's farm to spend Thanksgiving Day,
    Where grown-ups would visit and the children all would play.

The drive was always pleasant. There was so much to see.
    My father always pointed out bits of history.

He told us all the stories about the farms that we drove by.
    Having all that knowledge, to him, was a source of pride.

When we arrived at my Uncle's farm, we all helped unload the car.
    Our bodies were somewhat stiff and sore; not used to driving that far.

When you visited my Uncle's farm, it was like traveling
    back in time. The sights and smells of that place will linger in your mind.

There were people scrambling everywhere, trying to get things
    done. My Uncle grabbed me by the arm and said "Please Follow me son."

I followed him outside, this man of six-foot-two;
    He turned around to look at me and said, "There are chores to do."

So, I gathered up the eggs the best that I knew how.
    Then I slopped the hogs, fed the sheep, and even milked the cow.

I took the basket of eggs inside the house to proclaim that I was
    done. My Uncle looked at me and said, "Boy, you've just begun."

He took me back outside and I did the rest of the chores;
    Praying, when I walked inside, that he would have no more.

When I walked up to the farmhouse, he met me at the door.
    I asked him how I did. He said, "From a man, I could ask
    no more."

Then I walked into the dining room. The table was all set.
    The smell of country cooking, I never will forget.

Then, I stood there by the old wood stove to warm my hands
    and feet. With food now on the table, everything was now
    complete.

We all sat around the table and bowed our heads to pray.
    My Uncle thanked the Lord for all the family gathered
    here today.

We all ate dressing, turkey, and potatoes, until we could eat no
    more. The cat even had a good meal from the scraps he ate
    from the floor.

With the meal all finally finished, I followed the men outside.
    They bragged about the cooking and gently rubbed their sides.

With the day almost over and night time coming fast,
    I clung on the moment and tried to make it last.

Thanksgiving was almost over for another year.
    Would this happen again; would everyone still be here?

I guess I just don't know, I don't think ahead that far.
    My Dad hollered at me and I jumped into the car.

I left my Uncle's farm that night, knowing things were going to
    change, for no one lives forever, and nothing stays the same.

Memories Of Fall

I picked up my Dad the other day,
    he got in our car and we drove away.

It wasn't real special by any means,
    his work clothes were gone and replaced by his jeans.

As we headed from town I glanced at my side,
    my Dad looked so old but felt so alive.

For today was our day to do as we pleased,
    we walked through the woodlands and falling leaves.

My Dad was no talker, that you could say,
    but he showed that he loved us in so many ways.

By showing his son the heritage he had
    made me proud to call this man my Dad.

My Dad took us with him every Fall
    to walk the woodland and see it all.

From oak trees to creeks, I guess you could say,
    he taught us about life in so many ways.

But come this fall we'll walk it alone,
    the good Lord called and took him home.

But the memories made and the laughter we shared
    has proven to me just how much he cared.

A Prairie Town

On the flatlands of the prairie
    there sits a little town,
One that had its heyday,
    its share of ups and downs.

As you drive along its streets
    with its buildings new and old,
You sense there is a history here
    that someday must be told.

But for now I want to walk these streets
    and gaze into the stores,
And meet these special people
    who live behind these doors.

The people all were different,
    but their stories were all the same,
About how they came to live
    in this town without a name.

"Heritage," they said,
    drew us to this town.
My Father's Fathers roots are here;
    that's why we settled down

To live out on this prairie
    in this tiny little town.
Where everyone knows everyone
    for miles and miles around.

Then, suddenly it hit me
    as I walked out of the store,
This way of life is vanishing.
    One day it will be no more.

These people and this town,
    they are a dying breed.
Progress will end this way of life;
    in that we all agree.

Signs Of The Season

Fall is upon us;
    there is a coolness in the air.
Leaves of golden yellow
    are falling everywhere.

People are raking yards
    and canning time is here.
This has always been
    my favorite time of year.

Kids are carving pumpkins,
    Halloween's around the bend.
It makes me think back
    to when I was young again.

Vegetables were picked from the garden;
    harvest was at hand.
Farmers were busy
    all throughout the land.

The fall of the year is special
    in many splendid ways.
Come the month of November,
    we stop, give thanks and praise.

Then when winter finally settles in
    and fall's no longer here,
The only choice we're given
    is to wait another year.

The Silent Train

Can you hear that whistle blow,
    it's calling to me again,
Like some ghost from the past
    who wants to be my friend.

I can still see that train
    as it used to roll into town.
It's a memory of my past that today
    would not be found.

As kids we used to sit
    and watch the cars fill up with grain.
Then we played conductor;
    we were the man who drove the train.

Together we grew up,
    young children with the memories of trains.
Then one day long ago it happened;
    it was something strange.

The whistle became silent; the trains,
    they were no more.
History came and took them
    and slowly closed the door.

A big part of our life disappeared
    with those trains,
And somehow deep inside,
    I knew we would never be the same.

We grew up to be young gentlemen,
    our lives forever changed.
But our memories live on
    at the sound of a whistling train.

A Treasured House

On a quiet little street on a corner lot
    there sits a little house that sure has seen a lot.

The color of the house is white with trim of darkest green.
    The kind of house you'd picture somewhere in a dream.

The family that lives there moved in twenty years ago;
    together they've a history that all of you should know.

The house has always been there through the milestones of their lives,
Such as graduation, confirmation and the day the boys took their wives.

The house has been a friend to them through the passing years.
    It helped them through the rough times and soaked up all their tears.

This house has been a symbol when the kids took off to roam.
    No matter where they traveled, it's always been their home.

The old house sits so quiet now, the kids have moved away.
    My Mother lives there by herself; my Dad, he passed away.

But the memories of this house will linger in my mind.
    A treasure such as this in my life I'll maybe never find.

Changing Seasons

It was a beautiful fall day
    as I walked through the trees.
The ground was covered
    with red and golden leaves.
You could smell the dampness
    as it rose from the ground.
The birds that were singing
    made a sweet, pleasant sound.
I like to walk out here
    during this time of year.
It cleanses my soul
    and makes my head clear.
Seeing the seasons change
    in such a splendid way
Is God at his best;
    that you can say.
I am spending the day here
    just taking it all in.
Then, I think back to spring
    and how it begins.
What starts as a seed
    and then dies in the fall,
Should be a reminder
    to us one and all.
As the seasons change,
    so do our lives;
And we are all but a seed
    that will someday die.

Night Sounds

Have you walked outside your house at night
    and listened all around.
To how your world is put to sleep
    with all its different sounds?

The birds are singing everywhere,
    a perfect lullaby.
When the wind blows through the trees
    it almost makes you cry.

There's a quietness in the night
    just after it gets dark.
Somewhere in the distance
    you hear a dog begin to bark.

These sounds you hear most every night
    on any given day.
If only you would stop to hear
    what they had to say.

Fishing Daze

The sky was sunny and blue;
    the weather it was hot.
I sat along the shoreline
    and tied a granny knot.

The hook was baited with a worm
    and in the lake it went.
Fishing on an afternoon
    was how my day was spent.

I would lie back in the grass
    and gaze up to the sky.
The clouds were a picture
    that were pleasing to my eye.

You would watch the grass as it moved,
    swaying in the breeze.
And, the wind would sing a song
    as it rustled through the trees.

Days like this are etched
    deep inside my mind.
They are like a golden treasure
    that is getting hard to find.

For the days that we're living
    are not like the days of old.
That's why our memories of our youth
    must somehow now be told.

When Life Unfolds

My best friend died
    I heard yesterday.

The good Lord called
    and took him away.

The person he was
    and dreams that we shared

Are gone for now.
    My life is so bare.

The death of a friend
    seems to be so unfair;

It makes you wonder
    why should I care.

But life is funny
    the way it unfolds,

The length of our stay,
    we are never told.

So, live life to the fullest
    and cherish each day.

And, always remember
    to stop and say, "I love you."

The Gift

There was no money for Christmas this year;
    so I took my pen in hand.
For the gift that I am writing you
    is from your loving man.

If dreams are for the dreamers
    and love is for the lovers,
Then you were meant for me
    and I shall have no other.

Fate threw us together
    to share our lives as one.
Up and down the road of life,
    we'll finish what we've begun.

It started as a spark,
    then turned into a flame.
Suddenly, we were married
    and you were given my last name.

I will never give you much in life;
    it's just the way it will be.
I was made for you
    and you were made for me.

Then, let's join our hands together
    and walk the road of life.
And, cherish every moment
    that we are man and wife.

Hill of Dreams

I walked up to the hill; it's still the best place to sit.
    The memory of this time and place, I never will forget.

It all started back in my younger days; that's where I shall begin.
    I was always the odd one; I never quite fit in.

To say I was a dreamer, is a fact, my Father would say.
    I could sit forever and dream the day away.

Then one afternoon I took off for a drive that I remember still,
    cruising down that dusty road and seeing that grassy hill.

I parked along the road; then crossed the barbed-wire fence.
    I cut my hand that day and have carried a scar with me since.

Then I walked on through the prairie grass that grew throughout the field.
It was acting like some armor for that tiny hill.

Then I found an old cow trail that led me up that hill.
    When I reached the top, it seemed like time was standing still.

There were flowers on the hillside growing everywhere.
    The beauty of that moment wiped away all my cares.

Then I sat down on that boulder that had stood the test of time.
    It was an ancient piece of history that forever was all mine.

I gazed across the prairie to see what I could see.
    I saw plots of fields and farms and acres and acres of trees.

I sat there as the dreamer, dreaming of things to come,
    wasting away the day waiting for the setting sun.

I sat there on the boulder and felt the wind die down.
　With the colors of the setting sun, a better place could not
　be found.

With darkness almost upon me and the day forever done,
　I took one final look at the beautiful setting sun.

Then, I thought about this place and how I seemed to just fit in,
　standing on the hill and listening to the wind.

It seems I've searched forever and I'm glad that I could find,
　This little piece of heaven that God had left behind.

Childhood Memories

There is a place where I can go
    when the world's too much for me.
A place I'm always welcomed,
    called my childhood memories.

The days of playing
    "Kick the Can" and "Alai Oxen Free"
Are things that I remember
    and take through life with me.

The hot days of July,
    and the Indian summers too,
Help to remind me of the things
    we used to do.

Like riding bikes through our town
    is something we all did.
The swimming pool and baseball
    were the stuff we did as kids.

So if you see me standing
    with a look that's far away,
I won't be gone for long;
    I just went back there to play.

Take Time

I got up in a hurry to start the brand new day.
    No time to talk to Dad, I was on my way.

I got to school on time, then thought on what I did;
    The stupid things you say and do when you are just a kid.

I brushed him off again, no time to talk to Dad,
    He was looking kind of hurt and a little sad.

So many times we hurry, never stopping to say "Hi"
    And every time we do, the time will pass you by.

So many times I think about the things I never did,
    Wishing I could have changed things back when I was a kid.

For life is too short to live it like this;
    Suddenly, I realized just what I had missed.

My Dad wanted more than a casual, "Hi;"
    He wanted conversation, not a wave and goodbye.

So next time that you see your Dad, stop and talk awhile,
    Have a conversation and share a friendly smile.

For much too soon and to our dismay,
    The good Lord calls and takes them away.

Then all that is left of a son and his Dad
    Are memories like this. Won't you be glad?

Buddy Bunny

He was a stuffed bunny with yellow ears.
    He was my constant friend through my early years.

His overalls were white with spots of blue and red.
    He came with me each night when I went to bed.

He kept me safe and warm each and every night.
    His warm fuzzy face I always saw at first light.

This bunny and I were friends; we would talk most every day.
    No one else could hear the words that he had to say.

Then, I awoke one morning to greet the brand new day,
    my bunny he just laid there; he did not want to play.

This went on through the morning and then on through the week.
    My bunny was silent, no words did he speak.

At first I was mad, this could not be.
    Why wouldn't my bunny talk to me?

Then all at once it hit me from out of the blue.
    My bunny was not real, that I never knew.

I guess that I was growing up; I'd have no need for toys like this.
    Maybe I was right, but I know I am going to miss

The way he would listen when no one else was around.
    A truer friend in life, I know shall not be found.

Winter Is Coming

The air was cool and crisp so I grabbed a coat to wear.
    I opened up the door and all I did was stare.

It had froze last night, frost was all around.
    It covered the trees and bushes in our little town.

I stepped off the porch, and walked down the street.
    The sight of this frost was truly hard to beat.

As the sun finally rose, it made the grass sparkle and shine.
    It made a picture that was pleasing to the eye and the mind.

By the time noon came, the frost had disappeared.
    Who would have known that it was even here.

No one I guess, but it left behind signs
    that winter was coming; it's not far behind.

So cherish these days of the early fall,
    because when the seasons change you'll want to recall

The way things looked, the sights and sounds
    of the place you call your home town.

Growing Older

I looked into the mirror;
    I'm growing older every day.
Time will not stand still for me
    no matter what I say.

I'm looking back at my life
    to where it all begun.
I see the mistakes that I have made
    and things I've left undone.

I won't complain about my life;
    I won't complain you see.
Every choice I've ever made
    was made by only me.
For when I started out in life,
    I was lonely as I could be.

I met my wife one starry night
    many years ago.
And, from that bond of love,
    we've watched two children, grow.

We watched them grow
    from babies to toddlers at three.
Suddenly, they are teenagers
    looking a bit like me.

Oh yes, I'm growing older
    and I hope it stays that way.
For I want to live long enough to hear,
    "Grandpa can we play?"

Best Friends

The little boy had black hair; he was quiet and so shy.
    I walked on over to him and said a friendly, "HI."

We talked a lot that day about the things we know.
    Suddenly, the school bell rang and it was time to go.

Through each passing grade our friendship grew each day.
    A bond of trust was growing in many different ways.

Our parents taught us well about the meaning of a friend.
    They will always stick beside you to the very end.

The day we graduated we both knew in our minds
    that lives would change forever; New friends we'd have
to find.

We kept in touch throughout the years, but it was not the same.
    The two of us took our brides and gave them our last names.

Oh yes, the years are many now, and hair is turning gray.
    We're looking so much older then we did yesterday.

But when you stop and think what we all have been through,
    a greater friend I'll never find; I'm glad that friend was you.

Grandma's House

When I think back of my childhood,
    of another place in time,
I think of Grandma's house
    in the summer time.

The house was old and rustic;
    it was weathered, you could see.
It filled my youthful years
    with a flood of memories.

Memories of people
    and the things we always did;
That house made life
    so special when I was just a kid.

Cousins, aunts, and uncles
    were always a familiar face;
Having coffee in her kitchen
    seemed to be "the place."

The front porch in the afternoon
    was a cool, comfortable place.
You could see it by the smiles
    on everybody's face.

Then, come the evening hours,
    and the table was all set.
We would all eat supper together;
    It's hard to forget

The sights, sounds, and smells
    that old house would make.
Memories of another time
    are truly hard to shake.

Christmas Time

Picture if you can, a cold December night.
    The snow is falling softly; the moon is shining bright.

Carolers are walking down the street and music fills the air.
    Families are together; there is love and peace everywhere.

I remember scenes like this, they are of long ago
    of Christmas time and presents and hoping it would snow.

But now the times are changing; they are different as can be.
    No one knows who Santa is, and what's a Christmas tree?

Christmas has become as commercial as can be.
    I know it could be different, if only we believe

That Christmas time is truly about the birth of a Child,
    born in a manger, so meek and mild.

So, come this Christmas, please help me if you can
    Try to love your neighbor and help your fellow man.

Then, maybe we can start to see the scene of long ago,
    of Christmas time and presents, and hoping it would snow.

Proud Farmers

You can tell that they are farmers by their weathered tans.
    Their skin is tough as leather; there are calluses on their hands,
From working on the farm and planting crops across the land.

They're an icon of America that time is passing by;
    slowly, one by one, we watched their farms up and die.

For the times, they are a changing; they're not like the days of old.

So, before they are forgotten, their stories must be told,

About how the family farm has been passed down through the years.

And, how they kept it in the family name through blood, sweat, and tears.

They never had much money, but the kids were always fed.
    They showed them what a family is, and tucked them in each night to bed.

They're farmers and they're proud of it. You can see it by their smiles, and by the way they help their neighbors and go that extra mile.

Now, I hope America wakes up soon, before there's too much harm, to save that icon of America called the family farm.

Our Futures

Growing up as a kid, we would dream of things to come.
    What would our lives be like when childhood years were done?

Would our lives be like the ones our parents had?
    Would I turn out to be a person somewhat like my Dad?

These were questions never answered.
    There always was some doubt.

No one knew for sure what life was all about.
    Their lives will be a struggle; they will do the best they can.

Girls will grow to ladies and a boy to be a man.
    Somewhere down the line, when they live to be very old, they will try to teach their children the lessons they were told.

But like the ones before them, they will learn it on their own.
    This lesson called life on the day that they leave home.

The Duck Hunt

He was just an old hunter, truly past his prime.
  He was sorting through the memories that were drifting through his mind,
Tomorrow was almost here, the time had finally come.
  He was passing on his heritage to his youngest son.
It was just some old decoys and a weathered old shotgun.
  They would spend the day hunting ducks, hoping to have some fun.
The Father was the first to rise, then woke his son from bed.
  He was still tired and sleepy; cobwebs filled his head.
But today was the day the season had begun.
  They were now in a race to beat the rising sun.
They got into their pickup and headed out of town.
  Darkness was upon them; they could barely see the ground.
When they reached the farmer's slew, Father said, "it's not that far."
  It felt like we had walked for miles since we left the car.
They were walking through the muck and mud when the boy slipped and fell.
He got back up and quickly announced, "These ducks can go to hell."
The Father turned around and grinned, then said, "We're almost there."
The son was losing hope, and he really did not care.
Then the Father entered the slew to set the decoys up,
  and turned around to his son and quietly said, "Shut up."
The ducks are going to hear you; they never will appear.
  Son, I know you're cold, but the time is almost here.

Then he walked back to the blind and sat beside his son.
The young boy thought to himself, "How can he find this fun."

They sat here in the darkness and watched the daylight appear.
Then the boy looked at his Father and saw a single tear.

The boy asked of his Father, "Why do you shed those tears."
The Father looked toward his Son and said, "My day is almost here."

Then they watched the sunrise with it's colors of orange, blue and red.
A picture of that sunrise was etched deep inside their heads.

And then the ducks flew in right on cue.
They shot the sky full of holes and managed to drop a few.

Then, the son looked at his Father and said, with a great big grin, "Hey Dad, this was fun, when can we do this again."

With that, the Father's job was complete, he had passed it down to his son.
It was just a bunch of old decoys and a weathered old shotgun.

Love's Mistake

The doctor said the tests are back
    and there's a baby on the way.
The girl hung her head in silence,
    there was nothing she could say.

She had just turned sixteen;
    her life was now a mess.
The doctor asked, "Should I call your folks?"
    The girl just whispered, "yes."

How could this have happened?
    I took precautions, so did he.
But, the baby was the proof,
    something had gone wrong indeed.

Then her Mom walked in the room
    and sat down on the chair.
The daughter told her story
    of this boy who really cared.

About one night long ago,
    their love just couldn't wait.
Now she must pay the price
    for one night of love's mistake.

Give it up, or keep it?
    Should I drop out of school?
Everyone is sure to think
    that I am such a fool.

I guess I am the fool
    to let passion rule my life.
By the time I turn seventeen,
    will I be a wife?

One night of love's mistake
    will haunt me the rest of my days.
I guess it must be true,
    that abstinence is the only way.

My Little Girl

If there's one moment in my life that I'll remember until the
    day I die,
It was the first time, as a man, someone saw me cry.

I was sitting by my wife holding her tiny hand;
    looking into her eyes and thinking "Isn't life just grand."

The doctor said, "It's time," then, "Congratulations! It's a girl."
    Just for one brief moment, time stood still in our world.

The doctor wrapped her up and put her in my arms.
    I vowed that day to God to protect her from all harm.

But as babies grow, so do their dreams.
    In the blink of an eye, she grew from diapers to blue jeans.

She was growing up fast in a dangerous world.
    but in the eyes of her Dad, she'll always be his little girl.

The Childhood Swing

The gunny sack and rope
    were dangling from a tree.
The sack filled with straw
    made a swing just for me.

Growing up as a child,
    it meant the world to me.
It took me on adventures
    that no one else could see.

The swing was a teacher;
    it taught us everyday
how to play with others
    and watch the words we say.

The swing has always been there
    hanging from that tree.
It made the world in which I lived
    a special place to be.

As I drove by my old house
    just the other day,
The memories of my youth
    called me back to play.

But standing back
    and seeing that swing all alone,
Made me miss my childhood
    and the place that I called home.

It's funny now, as I look back
    at the memories of that swing.
All the things I learned
    there never cost a thing.

Sundays

The church bell rang so loud and clear
    to greet the brand new day.
Sundays in a small town
    always seem to start this way.

People hurry off
    to get to church on time;
A scene I know I have lived
    at least a thousand times.

Sundays in a small town
    are quiet and serene.
They are the kind of day
    you might picture in a dream.

Where you walk the streets of the town,
    where the people all are friends,
And where the "HI's" and waves,
    "Hello" never seem to end.

The smell of Sunday cooking
    floats along in the breeze,
And the sound of children laughing
    is heard rustling through the leaves.

Yes, Sundays in a small town
    are special in many ways.
If only we could have them
    each and every day.

Time Together

I got up in the morning, just like all the days before,
    I grabbed myself some breakfast and walked outside the door.

The sun, it was a shinin'; the sky was sunny blue,
    The grass, it was still wet from the morning dew.

I stood there on the porch and felt the morning breeze,
    The smell of pine was drifting' from the trees.

I turned around to ask my son, "Isn't this a perfect day?"
    He nodded with a smile, and we were on our way.

The fishing poles and tackle were put neatly in the truck;
    We stood there for a moment and prayed for a little luck.

We drove out on the highway; excitement filled the air;
    A father and a son goin' fishin' without a care.

When we got to Deerfield, and stood beside the shore
    The water was smooth as glass; "Who could ask for more?"

As we baited up our hooks, I caught Josh's nervous smile.
    Quietly he asked me, "Dad, can we talk awhile?"

We sat there on the bank, just my son and me.
    The poles were in their holders; our backs against a tree.

The worms they get a reprieve; my son he wants to talk.
    We brushed dirt off our backsides and took a little walk.

He told about his week, how things were in school,
    How a girl he thought was special made him feel just like a fool.

Then we talked about his future and what he dreamed he'd be,
I was quite surprised when he said someone like me!

Well, we walked back to our truck and sat there for a while,
No fish were caught this outing; you'd not know it by
his smile.

When we got home, my wife asked, "Did you do some good
today?"
I grinned at Josh and answered, "It was a perfect day."

Lonely and Forgotten

He was just an old man, sitting on a park bench by himself.
    He looked like a forgotten doll placed high upon a shelf.

The world was rushing by him, and people were too,
    as I made my way through the crowd to say, "How do you do,"

He sadly looked up at me, and said, "Can you sit for awhile."
    I took the seat next to him and saw him start to smile.

He said, "I know I am old and way past my prime,"
    and the world has forgotten me like some old worn dime.

"But, thank you for stopping to talk to me today,
    because visits like this help to pass the time away."

Then I asked "Why are you sitting here by your self all alone.
    Don't you have a family, a place that you call home?"

He said, "I used to many year's ago,
    but most of my family is gone. The rest I hardly know.

Then they put me in this home and said it was for the best.
    They said I'd fit right in cause I was just like all the rest.

But, I'm not you know I'm different, different as can be.
    Why can't they look past my age and see that I'm still me?"

Then I saw a tear that was running down his face,
    and I felt less than kind about the human race.

How could we do this to people so kind?
    Has the world gone mad? Have we lost our mind?

Then he said to get along now, You have better things to do.

You've wasted too much time with me. What else could I do?

I walked away from the bench and was back in the crowd, thinking of his story, and what had happened to a man so proud.

Then I turned around to thank him, for the visit that we had and to say no time was wasted, that I was more than glad.

To spend some time with him just to let him know I care, and glad that we have a memory now that both of us can share.

Growing Pains

I stormed out of the house. I said "It's just not fair.
    Is anybody listening? Does someone really care?

I was all of fourteen, and the world was rushing by;
    I was so confused, I bowed my head to cry.

I tried to tell my parents that I finally had arrived,
    and I was now an adult. I said it with such pride.

My parents shook their heads. You've got growing left to do.
    Don't be so impatient. Time will wait for you.

Then I blew my top with anger and nasty words were said.
    I hate the both of you. I wish you both were dead.

I ran outside the door, confused as I could be.
    Tears filled my eyes and it was getting hard to see.

Then I felt this presence, it was my Father by my side.
    He wrapped his arms around me, and he began to cry.

I know your life's not easy; there's changes you're going through.
    But parenting is tough; it's confusing for us, too.

Just try to remember, no matter what you say or do,
    That we will always be your parents. Just remember we love you.

Graduation

Graduation is finally over, my new life has begun.
    I stand here on the threshold looking back at what I
    have done.

Then, my thoughts turn towards the future, for I am now a man.
    It's time that I leave home to make my way the best I can.

That night before I left home I sat there on my bed.
    Lord I could not sleep, too many thoughts were in my head.

I thought about my parents, my family, and my friends.
    When I leave this town, will I ever see them again?

Then I thought about tomorrow and when I say goodbye.
    Will I play it tough, or will I start to cry?

I sat there in the darkness in my room all alone,
    wondering if when I leave, could I still call this place
    my home.

Then someone opened up my door; it was my Father I could see.
    He walked into my room and sat there next to me.

He spoke not a word; as he sat there by my side.
    Suddenly, he looked at me, and he began to cry.

He said, "It's time I do my crying, and when it's said and done,
    I want to hug my youngest, and tell him 'job well done.'"

In all the years I can remember, I'd never seen my Father cry.
    His youngest was now leaving home, that must be the
    reason why.

He said I was his favorite and it was hard to let me go.
    Then I hugged my Dad that night, and said, "I love you so."

When I went to bed that night, I fell asleep with a sense of pride.
    I had learned my first lesson as a man, that it was all right
    to cry.

Paying a Visit

She was just an old lady who lived all alone
    in a tiny apartment, a place that she called home.

The last time that I saw her was in my high school days.
    She hadn't changed a bit, but I had in many ways.

When I knocked on her door, she opened it wide.
    She seemed somewhat startled and a bit surprised.

She stepped back and shook her head and said, "I don't believe
    my eyes."
With those few words spoken, we both began to cry.

I sat down on her couch and we talked of days long ago,
    About the people and places that we both would know.

Then, I asked her about her age. She said, "I'm ninety-three,
    The rest of the family is gone now, I guess it's only me.

All my friends I ever knew have died and gone before."
    On that sad note, I stood up and walked on over to the door.

The time had come for me to go, but I said, "I'll stop again.
    Then she shook my hand and smiled the smile of a friend.

Then, I walked outside her door and stood there for a while,
    I was thinking of my old friend and her gentle, friendly smile.

Then, I thought to myself, I hope, when her life is at an end,
    That the Lord will take her home to be back with her
    old friends.

A Brother's Friend

I was born the youngest in a family of three.
    My brother was the oldest and he looked out for me.

From the time I learned to walk, he's been there by my side
    Guiding my every step with a watchful eye.

He's always been a friend, when friends were hard to find.
    He's been my big brother when I was less than kind.

He was my constant shadow through the perils of my life.
    He was my best man when I married my wife.

I know there will come a time when I will want to repay
    My brother for his wisdom that he taught me every day.

But for now I want to stop so you can hear me say,
    "Thank you, brother, for showing me the way."

And somewhere down the road when his life is at an end,
    He'll know the pleasure of heaven for being a brother's friend.

Nothing Stays The Same

If I have learned anything in life,
    it is nothing stays the same.
Our lives are constantly changing;
    no one is to blame.

Babies are born
    and people die;
I have no answer
    to the reason why.

We are granted
    new life every day,
then in a blink of an eye
    someone is taken away.

The world does not stop
    when a baby is born,
But is does for death
    so that we may mourn.

We mourn the loss
    of a cherished friend;
We grieve a little
    but it must end.

Then after a while
    baby is born.
It's time to rejoice
    and not to mourn.

We should rejoice in new life
    each and every day,
And hold fast to the memories
    of those taken away.

What Happens to Your Prayers?

Have you ever stopped to wonder,
    what happens to your prayers,
When it leaves your lips,
    and floats out in the air?

They say that someone's watching us;
    they say that someone cares.
As Christians,
    we believe that God is everywhere.

But sometimes when we're troubled
    it's hard to believe
In something without a shape or form
    that we cannot see.

So if seeing is believing
    then we must feel with our hearts.
I was told long ago,
    it is the best place to start.

So next time you are troubled
    and don't know what to do,
Give your heart to Jesus;
    He's waiting there for you.

Frank and Jetta Schwader, parents of Joel David Schwader.

I Know She Misses Dad
(Dedicated to Jetta Schwader)

I know she misses Dad,
>   I can see it in her eyes.
Her lips they will tremble,
>   but Lord she will not cry.

To us kids, she is a loving Mom
>   now living all alone
In a house she shared with Dad;
>   a place that they called home.

She says that everything is different now,
>   she says it with a smile.
The hardest part is living alone,
>   that she says, will take a while.

The cooking now seems harder
>   when your cooking just for one,
And eating by yourself,
>   how could anyone find that fun.

Then there's the yard to cut in the summer
>   and snow in the winter time;
The hardship she is enduring,
>   is always on my mind.

How could the Lord separate
>   this man from this wife
And make things so difficult
>   as she walks the road of life.

But the Lord knows best
>   and there's a lesson to be learned.
Always cherish your loved one
>   before it becomes your turn.

Someone's Missing

The house where I was born
    is a house to me no more.
Suddenly, it was different,
    as I walked through the door.

The pictures, lamps, and books
    all seem to be in place.
But, suddenly I realized
    it's missing a familiar face.

I walked into the kitchen;
    the smells all stayed the same.
But somehow, someone's missing;
    I do not know their name.

The living room is different,
    it's quiet as a mouse.
Then suddenly, I realized
    it's that way throughout the house.

Something here is different,
    it does not seem the same.
When, all at once, I woke up
    and realized his name.

My Father passed away,
    it happened yesterday.
All the pain and all the hurt,
    it will not go away.

So, I came inside this house
    to walk upon these floors,
To feel my father's presence,
    if only for once more.

My Church

I stood outside the church, and the door swung open wide.
    The preacher man, he asked me to please come on inside.

I walked inside the church and I sat down in the pew.
    It had been so long, I didn't know what to do.

So, I did like all the rest and bowed my head to pray.
    I was there to talk to Jesus, but I didn't know what to say.

So I sat there in the silence, when I felt this feeling deep inside.
    It was a happy one; it almost made me cry.

There were no words to speak, for I had forgotten how to pray.
    Why then, could you tell me, was I feeling this way?

I guess it must be true the Lord works in mysterious ways.
    He had touched this sinners heart and I didn't even pray.

A Hero

I came home from work and the news was on t.v.
    Day by day it's getting worse, or maybe it's just me.

Children killing children and parents who just don't care,
    In the small town's and the cities, it's happening everywhere.

They say it's just the times; it's the world we're living in.
    I believe it's time to change, but were just to begin,

We could start with a hero, like the ones in the good old days;
    He could bring back some morals, to help us find our way,

He wouldn't have to do commercials or endorsement's or the ads,
    Just have a good heart, and be someone like my dad.

He wouldn't have to be rich or famous or a t.v. super star.
    He could be the kind of person, who likes you just the way you are,

He would be the kind of hero to put America back on her feet,
    He'd be clean cut and wholesome with values hard to beat.

But people like this are hard to find in these troubled times;
    There has to be someone out there that we could find.

Someone in the nineties who believes in just this way
    Who wants to take America back to the good old days.

The Blacksmith

He was a blacksmith by trade, a relic lost in time,
    In the early years of my life, he became a friend of mine.

Although I was barely eleven, too young to understand,
    One sunny afternoon I learned a lesson from this man.

He was busy stoking coals, trying to get things done,
    When his friend stopped by and said, "I'd like you to meet my son."

Then he stopped what he was doing and talked to both of them,
    Twenty minutes later he waved good-bye to his old friend,

Then he went back to work, during the rest of the day,
    The old man was silent; he didn't have much to say,

Then about a quarter-to-five he started to close things down,
    When a friend showed up to visit, someone he knew from town,

Then he stopped again to visit and it was longer than before,
    An hour had gone by when he finally locked the door,

Then I said, "you must be crazy, you're trying to get things done,
    Why must you stop to visit and talk to everyone."

Then he looked real stern at me, then said, "Don't tell me what to do." Then he gave me some advice that I want to share with you.

He sat me on this stool and said, "Remember what I say."
    Thirty years have passed and I remember it yet today,

He said the value of your life is the moments that you live,
    It's the quality of friends you have and how much love you give,

I sat there, a young boy trying to understand,
    But nothing made sense to me, not even this old man,

It took me thirty years of living to finally understand,
    The lesson I was taught that day from that rough hewn man.

The Visit

The drive, it took an hour;
    it was made once a week.
    The old lady parked her car,
    for she had promises to keep.

Then she walked across the grass;
    she was here to see a friend,
    One she made a vow to love,
    forever without end.

When she saw his tombstone,
    she put the flowers on his grave.
    The morning turned to afternoon,
    as she bowed her head to pray,

I went out for a drive, and I saw
    her standing there,
    The weather had turned cold,
    but the lady did not care.

I stopped to see if she was fine,
    if there was something I could do,
    She said, "You look familiar son,
    I think I should know you.

Then she said, "You're the barber's son,
    he died a few years back,
    My how you've grown son,
    of time I just lost track."

She said her husband died,
    ten years ago today,
    Then I thought about my father,
    as I heard her start to say.

Gone but not forgotten are the people
   in these graves,
      In our minds they will live forever,
      in our hearts they'll always stay,

Then I put my arm around her,
   and said "It's time to go."
      Then she squeezed my hand real tight,
      and said, "I miss him so."

And as I helped her to her car,
   then watched her drive away,
      I walked on over to my dad,
      and stood beside his grave,

For I was feeling somewhat different;
   it came from deep inside,
      Peace filled my heart,
      no longer did I cry,

Her words they made sense to me,
   I'm glad I stopped today,
      to say good-bye to my dad,
      then slowly walked away.

A Treasured Friend

There was a treasure
    that I found a few years ago.
He was a husky gentleman
    with hair of silver and snow.

A love and passion for hunting
    paired us as friends.
We will hunt the prairie
    for sharptails to the very end.

The difference in our ages
    means nothing at all to me.
I am but a sapling, but he,
    a might oak tree.

The outlook that we share on life
    tends to run the same.
The only thing different between us
    is our last name.

The memories that we've made,
    the good times we've had
Has made me feel like I have been blessed
    with another Dad.

Uncle Paul

For as long as I can remember, back to the time that I was very small;
My Father always talked about his brother, that would be my Uncle Paul.

He talked about their lives, and how they lived back then;
And how Paul wasn't just his brother, he truly was his friend.

I heard stories of their trapping and the hunting that they did;
How money was hard to come by back when they were kids.

I heard the story of how their Father died when they were very small;
And how Uncle Ferdie did his best to try and feed them all.

Of all the stories that he told me, one thing always stayed the same;
That Dad and Paul were always proud to have the Schwader name.

A Tribute

When my Father passed away on September 3, 1996, I was totally unable to say "goodbye" at his funeral. It took me 15 months of learning to cope with his loss in order to finally come to terms with his death. I was eventually able to say "goodbye" in my own way with the following poem.

Writing my feelings down on paper allowed me to better cope with his death; this book of poems is to serve as a lasting tribute to my Father, the man who helped me to realize *The Things I Learned In Life*.

The Goodbye

I had a dream the other night that I crossed to the other side.
   I was standing there in heaven, the place where angels fly.

I looked around and said, "I know this cannot be;
   what would heaven want with someone like me."

Then, I heard a voice whispering; I heard it loud and clear.
   "Son, I know you're scared, but put away your fear."

I dropped down to my knees. I didn't know what to do.
   Then all at once, I looked up and saw that it was you.

My Father was just standing there; he said, "We need to talk."
   So, hand in hand in heaven, we took a little walk.

He said, "Tell your mom I'm doing fine; I'm feeling so much better.
   I wish she could be with me, if only they would let her.

I see that Todd and Dawn are getting by just fine.
   Tell them that I love them, and they're always on my mind.

Then, tell Josh and Melissa that I am with them every day.
   A part of me walks with them in many different ways.

As for you and my brother Paul, I have these words to say,
   I am sorry I did not say goodbye; there was no other way."

Then, Dad turned around and slowly walked away.
   He had answered all my questions; there was just one thing
   left to say.

I said my final goodbye and I meant it this time.
   I said, "Dad, you will live forever in our hearts and in
   our minds."

About the Author

Joel David Schwader was born in Madison, South Dakota on December 20, 1962. He resided the first five years in Howard, S.D. Joel and his family moved to Freeman, S.D. in 1967 when his father purchased a barber shop in that city. Joel attended both grade and high school in Freeman. In 1981, he met and fell in love with Kathy Herrlien. They were married on December 11, 1982. From that union their two children, Joshua and Melissa, were born. Joel and family presently reside in Custer, S.D. where they have lived for the past 12 years.

Well, there it is...... *The Things I Learned In Life.* It is my hope that you enjoyed reading this book of poems. It is my sincere wish that these poems might bring about a rekindling of your own life's special moments. It has been a pleasure sharing some of my life experiences with you on paper. I expect my interpretations of life to grow, thus providing me with additional material for my poems. I would enjoy hearing reader's comment on your likes and dislikes about my book. Your feedback would be gladly received at: 21 Pine Street, Custer, SD 57730. 605-673-5140

Yours truly,

Joel David Schwader
The Common Man's Poet

Special thanks to Gary and Marie Trusty for their countless hours dedicated to editing my book,

To my family, who never seemed to tire from listening to my poetry.

To all my friends whose words of encouragement about my poetry made this book possible

And to my father whose teaching helped me to learn *The Things I Learned In Life.*

Your spirit lives on,

Joel David Schwader
The Common Man's Poet